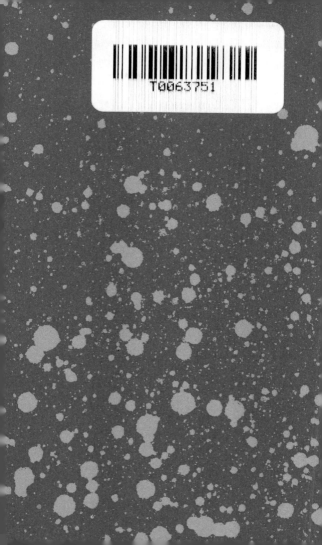

CAUTIONARY TALES

More poetry available from
Macmillan Collector's Library

ANTHOLOGIES

Poems About Birds ed. H. J. Massingham
Sunrise ed. Susie Gibbs
Happy Hour: Poems to Raise a Glass to introduced by Jancis Robinson
Poems for Stillness introduced by Ana Sampson
Poems of the Sea introduced by Adam Nicolson
Poems for Happiness introduced by Richard Coles
Poems for Travellers introduced by Paul Theroux
Poems for Christmas introduced by Judith Flanders
Poems of Childhood introduced by Michael Morpurgo
Poems on Nature introduced by Helen Macdonald
Poems for Love introduced by Joanna Trollope
Poems for New Parents ed. Becky Brown
The Golden Treasury ed. Francis Turner Palgrave
Poetry of the First World War ed. Marcus Clapham

COLLECTIONS

Goblin Market & Other Poems by Christina Rossetti
Leaves of Grass: Selected Poems by Walt Whitman
Selected Poems by John Keats
Poems of Thomas Hardy by Thomas Hardy
Collected Poems by W. B. Yeats
The Sonnets by William Shakespeare
Tales and Poems by Edgar Allan Poe
A Shropshire Lad by A. E. Housman
The Rime of the Ancient Mariner by Samuel Taylor Coleridge

HILAIRE BELLOC

CAUTIONARY TALES

Illustrated by
BASIL TEMPLE BLACKWOOD

MACMILLAN COLLECTOR'S LIBRARY

First published 1907

This edition first published 2024 by Macmillan Collector's Library
an imprint of Pan Macmillan
The Smithson, 6 Briset Street, London EC1M 5NR
EU representative: Macmillan Publishers Ireland Ltd,
1st Floor, The Liffey Trust Centre, 117–126 Sheriff Street Upper,
Dublin 1, D01 YC43
Associated companies throughout the world
www.panmacmillan.com

ISBN 978-1-0350-1740-9

The text of this book remains true to the original in every way and is reflective of the language and period in which it was originally written. Readers should be aware that there may be hurtful or indeed harmful phrases and terminology that were prevalent at the time this book was written and in the context of the historical setting of this book. Macmillan believes changing the text to reflect today's world would undermine the authenticity of the original, so has chosen to leave the text in its entirety. This does not, however, constitute an endorsement of the characterization, content or language used.

1 3 5 7 9 8 6 4 2

A CIP catalogue record for this book is available from the British Library.

Cover and endpaper design: Kieryn Tyler, Pan Macmillan Art Department
Printed and bound in China by Imago

Contents

MORE BEASTS FOR WORSE CHILDREN

CAUTIONARY TALES FOR CHILDREN

INTRODUCTION

Upon being asked by a Reader whether the verses contained in this book were true.

And is it True? It is not True.
And if it were it wouldn't do,
For people such as me and you
Who pretty nearly all day long
Are doing something rather wrong.
Because if things were really so,
You would have perished long ago,
And I would not have lived to write
The noble lines that meet your sight,
Nor B. T. B. survived to draw
The nicest things you ever saw.

H. B.

Jim,

Who ran away from his Nurse, and was eaten by a Lion.

There was a Boy whose name was Jim;
His Friends were very good to him.
They gave him Tea, and Cakes, and Jam,
And slices of delicious Ham,
And Chocolate with pink inside,
And little Tricycles to ride,
And

read him Stories through and through,
And even took him to the Zoo—
But there it was the dreadful Fate
Befell him, which I now relate.

You know—at least you *ought* to know,
For I have often told you so—
That Children never are allowed
To leave their Nurses in a Crowd;

Now this was Jim's especial Foible,
He ran away when he was able,
And on this inauspicious day
He slipped his hand and ran away!
He hadn't gone a yard when—

Bang!
With open Jaws, a Lion sprang,
And hungrily began to eat
The Boy: beginning at his feet.

Now just imagine how it feels
When first your toes and then your heels,
And then by gradual degrees,
Your shins and ankles, calves and knees,
Are slowly eaten, bit by bit.

No wonder Jim detested it!
No wonder that he shouted "Hi!"
The Honest Keeper heard his cry,
Though very fat

he almost ran
To help the little gentleman.
"Ponto!" he ordered as he came
(For Ponto was the Lion's name),
"Ponto!" he cried,

with angry Frown.
"Let go, Sir! Down, Sir! Put it down!"

The Lion made a sudden Stop,
He let the Dainty Morsel drop,
And slunk reluctant to his Cage,
Snarling with Disappointed Rage
But when he bent him over Jim,
The Honest Keeper's

Eyes were dim.
The Lion having reached his Head,
The Miserable Boy was dead!

When Nurse informed his Parents, they
Were more Concerned than I can say:—
His Mother, as She dried her eyes,
Said, "Well—it gives me no surprise,
He would not do as he was told!"
His Father, who was self-controlled,
Bade all the children round attend

To James' miserable end,
And always keep a-hold of Nurse
For fear of finding something worse.

Henry King,

Who chewed bits of String, and was early cut off in Dreadful Agonies.

The Chief Defect of Henry King
Was

chewing little bits of String.
At last he swallowed some which tied

Itself in ugly Knots inside.

Physicians of the Utmost Fame
Were called at once; but when they came
They answered,

as they took their Fees,
"There is no Cure for this Disease.
Henry will very soon be dead."
His Parents stood about his Bed
Lamenting his Untimely Death,
When Henry, with his Latest Breath,
Cried—

"Oh, my Friends, be warned by me,

That Breakfast, Dinner, Lunch and Tea
Are all the Human Frame requires . . ."
With that the Wretched Child expires.

Matilda,

Who told Lies, and was Burned to Death.

Matilda told such Dreadful Lies,

It made one Gasp and Stretch one's Eyes;
Her Aunt, who, from her Earliest Youth,
Had kept a Strict Regard for Truth,

Attempted to Believe Matilda:
The effort very nearly killed her,
And would have done so, had not She
Discovered this Infirmity.
For once, towards the Close of Day,
Matilda, growing tired of play,

And finding she was left alone,
Went tiptoe

to

the Telephone
And summoned the Immediate Aid
Of London's Noble Fire-Brigade.
Within an hour the Gallant Band
Were pouring in on every hand,
From Putney, Hackney Downs and Bow,
With Courage high and Hearts a-glow
They galloped, roaring through the Town,

"Matilda's House is Burning Down!"
Inspired by British Cheers and Loud
Proceeding from the Frenzied Crowd,
They ran their ladders through a score
Of windows on the Ball Room Floor;
And took Peculiar Pains to Souse
The Pictures up and down the House,

Until Matilda's Aunt succeeded
In showing them they were not needed
And even then she had to pay
To get the Men to go away!

★

It happened that a few Weeks later
Her Aunt was off to the Theatre
To see that Interesting Play

The Second Mrs. Tanqueray.

She had refused to take her Niece
To hear this Entertaining Piece:
A Deprivation Just and Wise
To Punish her for Telling Lies.
That Night a Fire *did* break out—
You should have heard Matilda Shout!
You should have heard her Scream and Bawl,

And throw the window up and call
To People passing in the Street—
(The rapidly increasing Heat
Encouraging her to obtain
Their confidence)—but all in vain!
For every time She shouted "Fire!"

They only answered "Little Liar!"
And therefore when her Aunt returned,

Matilda, and the House, were Burned.

Franklin Hyde,

Who caroused in the Dirt and was corrected by His Uncle.

His Uncle came on Franklin Hyde
Carousing in the Dirt.
He Shook him hard from Side to Side
And

Hit him till it Hurt,

Exclaiming, with a Final Thud,

"Take

that! Abandoned Boy!
For Playing with Disgusting Mud
As though it were a Toy!"

MORAL

From Franklin Hyde's adventure, learn
To pass your Leisure Time

In Cleanly Merriment, and turn
From Mud and Ooze and Slime
And every form of Nastiness—
But, on the other Hand,
Children in ordinary Dress
May always play with Sand.

Godolphin Horne,

Who was cursed with the Sin of Pride, and Became a Boot-Black.

Godolphin Horne was Nobly Born;
He held the Human Race in Scorn,
And lived with all his Sisters where
His father lived, in Berkeley Square.
And oh! the Lad was Deathly Proud!

He never shook your Hand or Bowed,
But merely smirked and nodded

thus:

How perfectly ridiculous!
Alas! That such Affected Tricks
Should flourish in a Child of Six!
(For such was Young Godolphin's age).

Just then, the Court required a Page,
Whereat

the Lord High Chamberlain
(The Kindest and the Best of Men),
He went good-naturedly and

took
A Perfectly Enormous Book
Called *People Qualified to Be*
Attendant on His Majesty,
And murmured, as he scanned the list
(To see that no one should be missed),
"There's

William Coutts has
got the Flue,

And Billy Higgs would never do,

And Guy

de Vere is far too young,

And . . . wasn't D'Alton's Father hung?
And as for Alexander Byng!— . . .
I think I know the kind of thing,
A Churchman, cleanly, nobly born,
Come

let us say Godolphin Horne?"
But hardly had he said the word
When Murmurs of Dissent were heard.
The King of Iceland's Eldest Son
Said, "Thank you! I am taking none!"
The Aged Duchess of Athlone
Remarked, in her sub-acid tone,
"I doubt if He is what we need!"
With which the Bishops all agreed;
And even Lady Mary Flood
(*So* Kind, and oh! so *really* good)
Said, "No! He wouldn't do at all,
He'd make us feel a lot too small."
The Chamberlain said,

"... Well, well, well!
No doubt you're right.... One cannot tell!"
He took his Gold and Diamond Pen
And

Scratched Godolphin out again.
So now Godolphin is the Boy

Who blacks the Boots at the Savoy.

Algernon,

Who played with a Loaded Gun, and, on missing his Sister was reprimanded by his Father.

Young Algernon,
the Doctor's Son,
Was

playing with a Loaded Gun.
He pointed it towards his sister,
Aimed very carefully, but

Missed her!

His Father, who
was standing near,

The Loud Explosion chanced to Hear,

And reprimanded Algernon
For playing with a Loaded Gun.

Hildebrand,

Who was frightened by a Passing Motor,
and was brought to Reason.

"Oh, Murder! What was that, Papa!"
"My child,

It was a Motor-Car,
A Most Ingenious Toy!

Designed to Captivate and Charm
Much rather than to rouse Alarm
In any English Boy.

"What would your Great Grandfather who

Was Aide-de-Camp to General Brue,

And lost a leg at

Waterloo,

And

Quatre-Bras and

Ligny too!

And died at Trafalgar!—

What would he have remarked to hear
His Young Descendant shriek with fear,
Because he happened to be near
A Harmless Motor-Car!
But do not fret about it! Come!

We'll off to Town

And purchase some!"

Lord Lundy,

Who was too Freely Moved to Tears, and thereby ruined his Political Career.

Lord Lundy from his earliest years
Was far too freely moved to Tears.
For instance if his Mother said,
"Lundy! It's time to go to Bed!"
He bellowed like a Little Turk.
Or if

his father Lord Dunquerque
Said "Hi!" in a Commanding Tone,
"Hi, Lundy! Leave the Cat alone!"
Lord Lundy, letting go its tail,
Would raise so terrible a wail
As moved

His
Grandpapa
the

Duke
To utter the severe rebuke:
"When I, Sir! was a little Boy,
An Animal was not a Toy!"

His father's Elder Sister, who
Was married to a Parvenoo,

Confided to Her Husband, "Drat!
The Miserable, Peevish Brat!
Why don't they drown the Little Beast?"
Suggestions which, to say the least,
Are not what we expect to hear
From Daughters of an English Peer.
His grandmamma, His Mother's Mother,

Who had some dignity or other,
The Garter, or no matter what,
I can't remember all the Lot!
Said "Oh! that I were Brisk and Spry
To give him that for which to cry!"
(An empty wish, alas! for she

Was Blind and nearly ninety-three).

The

Dear old Butler

thoughtc—but there!
I really neither know nor care
For what the Dear Old Butler thought!
In my opinion, Butlers ought
To know their place, and not to play
The Old Retainer night and day

I'm getting tired and so are you,
Let's cut the Poem into two!

★

Lord Lundy

(SECOND CANTO)

It happened to Lord Lundy then,
As happens to so many men:
Towards the age of twenty-six,
They shoved him into politics;
In which profession he commanded
The income that his rank demanded
In turn as Secretary for
India, the Colonies, and War.
But very soon his friends began
To doubt if he were quite the man:
Thus, if a member rose to say
(As members do from day to day),

"Arising out of that reply . . . !"

Lord Lundy would begin to cry.
A Hint at harmless little jobs
Would shake him with convulsive sobs.

While as for Revelations, these
Would simply bring him to his knees,
And leave him whimpering like a child.
It drove his Colleagues raving wild!
They let him sink from Post to Post,
From fifteen hundred at the most
To eight, and barely six—and then
To be Curator of Big Ben! . . .
And finally there came a Threat
To oust him from the Cabinet!

The Duke—his aged grand-sire—bore
The shame till he could bear no more.
He rallied his declining powers,
Summoned the youth to Brackley Towers,

And bitterly addressed him thus—
"Sir! you have disappointed us!
We had intended you to be
The next Prime Minister but three:
The stocks were sold; the Press was squared:
The Middle Class was quite prepared.
But as it is! . . . My language fails!

Go out and govern New South Wales!"

★

The Aged Patriot groaned and died:

And gracious! how Lord Lundy cried!

Rebecca,

Who slammed Doors for Fun and Perished Miserably.

A Trick that everyone abhors
In Little Girls is slamming Doors.
A

Wealthy Banker's

Little Daughter

Who lived in Palace Green, Bayswater
(By name Rebecca Offendort),
Was given to this Furious Sport.

She would deliberately go

And Slam the door
like Billy-Ho!

To make

her

Uncle Jacob start.
She was not really bad at heart,
But only rather rude and wild:
She was an aggravating child. . . .

It happened that a Marble Bust
Of Abraham was standing just
Above the Door this little Lamb
Had carefully prepared to Slam,
And Down it came! It knocked her flat!

It laid her out! She looked
like that.

★

Her funeral Sermon (which was long
And followed by a Sacred Song)
Mentioned her Virtues, it is true,
But dwelt upon her Vices too,

And showed the Dreadful End of One
Who goes and slams the door for Fun.

*

The children who were brought to hear
The awful Tale from far and near
Were much impressed,

and inly swore
They never more would slam the Door.
—As often they had done before.

George,

Who played with a Dangerous Toy, and suffered a Catastrophe of considerable Dimensions.

When George's Grandmamma was told

That George had been as good as Gold,
She Promised in the Afternoon
To buy him an *Immense BALLOON.*
And

so she did; but when it came,
It got into the candle flame,
And being of a dangerous sort
Exploded

with a loud report!

The Lights went out! The Windows broke!
The Room was filled with reeking smoke.
And in the darkness shrieks and yells
Were mingled with Electric Bells,
And falling masonry and groans,
And crunching, as of broken bones,
And dreadful shrieks, when, worst of all,
The House itself began to fall!
It tottered, shuddering to and fro,
Then crashed into the street below—
Which happened to be Savile Row.

★

When Help arrived, among the Dead
Were

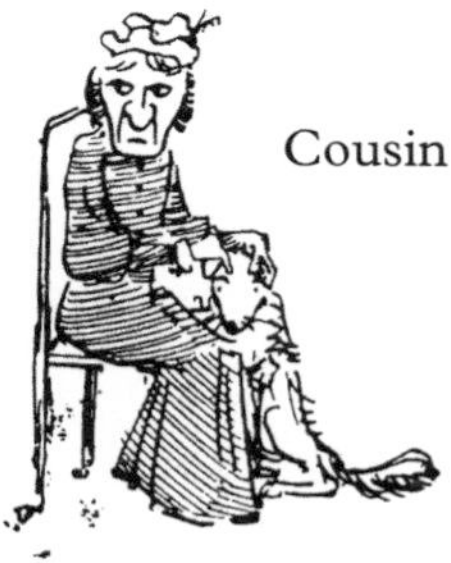

Cousin Mary,

Little Fred,

The Footmen

(both of them),

The Groom,

The man that cleaned the Billiard-Room,

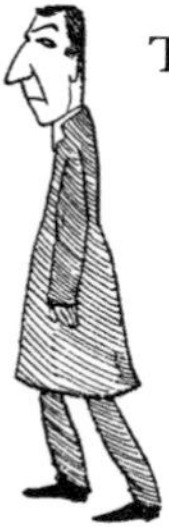

The Chaplain, and

The Still-Room Maid.

And I am dreadfully afraid
That Monsieur Champignon, the Chef,
Will now be

permanently deaf—

And both his

Aides

are much the same;
While George, who was in part to blame,
Received, you will regret to hear,
A nasty lump

behind the ear.

MORAL

The moral is that little Boys
Should not be given dangerous Toys.

Charles Augustus Fortescue,

Who always Did what was Right, and so accumulated an Immense Fortune.

The nicest child I ever knew
Was Charles Augustus Fortescue.
He never lost his cap, or tore
His stockings or his pinafore:
    In eating Bread he made no Crumbs,
    He was extremely fond of sums,

To which, however,
    he preferred
The Parsing of a
    Latin Word—
He sought, when it
    was in his power,
For information
    twice an hour,

And as for finding Mutton-Fat
Unappetising, far from that!
He often, at his Father's Board,
Would beg them, of his own accord,

To give him, if they did not mind,
The Greasiest Morsels they could find—
His Later Years did not belie
The Promise of his Infancy.

In Public Life he always tried
To take a judgment Broad and Wide;

In Private, none was more than he
Renowned for quiet courtesy.
He rose at once in his Career,
And long before his Fortieth Year
Had wedded

Fifi,

Only Child
Of Bunyan, First Lord Aberfylde.
He thus became immensely Rich,
And built the Splendid Mansion which
Is called

"The Cedars, Muswell Hill,"

Where he resides in Affluence still,
To show what Everybody might
Become by

SIMPLY DOING RIGHT.

THE BAD CHILD'S BOOK OF BEASTS

INTRODUCTION

I call you bad, my little child,
    Upon the title page,
Because a manner rude and wild
    Is common at your age.

The Moral of this priceless work
    (If rightly understood)
Will make you—from a little Turk—
    Unnaturally good.

Do not as evil children do,
    Who on the slightest grounds
Will imitate

    the Kangaroo,
With wild unmeaning bounds:

Do not as children badly bred,
    Who eat like little Hogs,
And when they have to go to bed
    Will whine like Puppy Dogs:

Who take their manners from the Ape,
    Their habits from the Bear,
Indulge the loud unseemly jape,
    And never brush their hair.

But so control your actions that
Your friends may all repeat.

'This child is dainty as the Cat,
And as the Owl discreet.'

The Yak

As a friend to the children

commend me the Yak.

You will find it exactly the thing:
It will carry and fetch,

you can ride on its back,

Or lead it about

with a string.

The Tartar who dwells on the plains of Thibet
(A desolate region of snow)

Has for centuries made it a nursery pet,
And surely the Tartar should know!

Then tell your papa where the Yak can be got,

And if he is awfully rich
He will buy you the creature—

or else

he will *not*.

(I cannot be positive which.)

The Polar Bear

The Polar Bear is unaware

Of cold that cuts me through:
For why? He has a coat of hair.
I wish I had one too!

The Lion

The Lion, the Lion, he dwells in the waste,
He has a big head and a very small waist;

But his shoulders are stark, and his jaws they
are grim,
And a good little child will not play with him.

The Tiger

The Tiger on the other hand,

is kittenish and mild,
He makes a pretty playfellow for any little child;
And mothers of large families (who claim to
common sense)

Will find a Tiger well repay the trouble and
expense.

The Dodo

The Dodo used

to walk around,

And take the sun and air.
The sun yet warms his native ground—

The Dodo is not there!

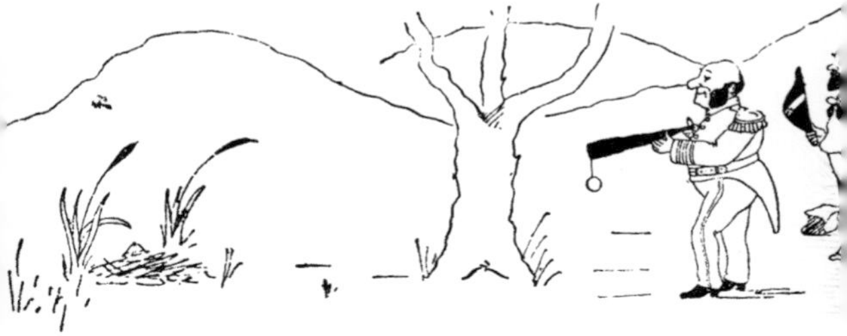

The voice which used to squawk and squeak
Is now for ever dumb—

Yet may you see his bones and beak
All in the Mu-se-um.

The Marmozet

The species Man and Marmozet
Are intimately linked;

The Marmozet survives as yet,
But Men are all extinct.

The Learned Fish

This learned Fish has not sufficient brains
To go into the water when it rains.

The Elephant

When people call this beast to mind,

They marvel more and more
At such a

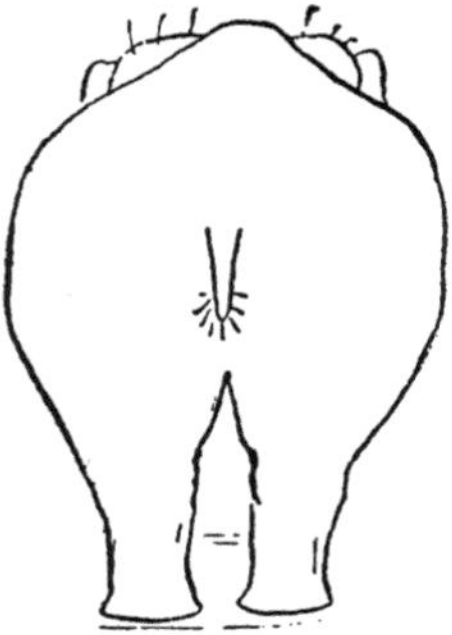

LITTLE tail behind,

So *LARGE* a trunk before.

The Rhinoceros

Rhinoceros, your hide looks all undone,

You do not take my fancy in the least:

You have a horn where other brutes have none:
Rhinoceros, you are an ugly beast.

MORE BEASTS
FOR WORSE CHILDREN

INTRODUCTION

The parents of the learned child
    (His father and his mother)
Were utterly aghast to note
The facts he would at random quote
On creatures curious, rare and wild;
    And wondering, asked each other:

"An idle little child like this,
How is it that he knows
What years of close analysis
Are powerless to disclose?

Our brains are trained, our books are big
And yet we always fail

To answer why the Guinea-pig
Is born without a tail.

Or why the Wanderoo* should rant
In wild, unmeaning rhymes,

* Sometimes called the "Lion-tailed or tufted Baboon of Ceylon."

Whereas the Indian Elephant
Will only read *The Times*.

Perhaps he found a way to slip
Unnoticed to the Zoo,
And gave the Pachyderm a tip,
Or pumped the Wanderoo.

Or even by an artful plan
Deceived our watchful eyes,
And interviewed the Pelican,
Who is extremely wise."

"Oh! no," said he, in humble tone,
With shy but conscious look,
"Such facts I never could have known
But for this little book."

The Python

A Python I should not advise,—
It needs a doctor for its eyes,
And has the measles yearly.

However, if you feel inclined
To get one (to improve your mind,
And not from fashion merely),
Allow no music near its cage;

And when it flies into a rage
Chastise it, most severely.

I had an aunt in Yucatan
Who bought a Python from a man
And kept it for a pet.
She died, because she never knew
These simple little rules and few;—

The Snake is living yet.

The Welsh Mutton

The Cambrian Welsh or Mountain Sheep
Is of the Ovine race,
His conversation is not deep,
But then—observe his face!

The Porcupine

What! would you slap the Porcupine ?
Unhappy child—desist!
Alas! that any friend of mine
Should turn Tupto-philist.*

* From τύπτω = I strike; φιλέω = I love; one that loves to strike. The word is not found in classical Greek, nor does it occur among the writers of the Renaissance—nor anywhere else.

To strike the meanest and the least
    Of creatures is a sin,

How much more bad to beat a beast
With prickles on its skin.

The Scorpion

The Scorpion is as black as soot,
He dearly loves to bite;
He is a most unpleasant brute
To find in bed, at night.

The Vulture

The Vulture eats between his meals,
And that's the reason why

He very, very rarely feels
As well as you and I.
His eye is dull, his head is bald,
His neck is growing thinner.
Oh! what a lesson for us all
To only eat at dinner!

The Bison

The Bison is vain, and (I write it with pain)
The Door-mat you see on his head

Is not, as some learned professors maintain,
The opulent growth of a genius' brain;

But is sewn on with needle and thread.

The Chamois

The Chamois inhabits
Lucerne, where his habits
(Though why I have not an idea-r)
Give him sudden short spasms
On the brink of deep chasms,
And he lives in perpetual fear.